Mitch Saves the Day

Story by Stephen Thraves

Based on the TV series, Fetch the Vet

Little Hippo

With thanks for technical help:
Suzanne Whight BVSc MRCVS
(Greenwood Veterinary Clinic, Chalfont St Peter)

Scholastic Children's Books,
Commonwealth House, 1-19 New Oxford Street,
London WC1A 1NU, UK
a division of Scholastic Ltd

London ~ New York ~ Toronto ~ Sydney ~ Auckland
Mexico City ~ New Delhi ~ Hong Kong

First published in the UK by Scholastic Ltd, 2000

Based upon the television series FETCH THE VET produced
by Flextech Rights Ltd and ITEL in association with Cosgrove Hall Films.
Original concept by Stephen Thraves and Gail Penston.

Text copyright © Stephen Thraves, 2000
Illustrations derived from FETCH THE VET television series,
copyright © Flextech Rights Ltd and ITEL, 2000.
Photographs by Jean-Marc Ferriere and Justin Nöe

ISBN 0 439 99731 3

Printed in Spain

All rights reserved

2 4 6 8 10 9 7 5 3 1

Tom Fetch the vet was on his way back to Duckhurst village. He had been looking forward to this day for weeks. Today was the day of the Duckhurst Village Pet Show and he was going to be the judge.

Fetch just had time to visit his friends at Whitecliff Farm before the show.

"Hello, Mr Fetch," called Joe as Fetch arrived. "You'll never guess who Lucy wants to enter in the pet show?"

At that very moment Lucy came running into the farm yard. She was chasing Trevor the goat and trying to put a ribbon on him.

"I'm going to ask Uncle George to take Trevor to the pet show!" said Lucy. "But I have to make him look pretty first."

Trevor did not want to look pretty. He honked the horn around his neck every time Lucy came near him with the ribbon.

"Poor Trevor!" Fetch chuckled to himself as he went to look for his friend, George. Fetch found George and Pippa, Lucy's sister, in one of the Whitecliff Farm fields.

"Hello George! Hello Pippa!" called Fetch.

"Look at Mitch!" Pippa said to Fetch excitedly. "Isn't he a clever sheepdog?"

"The cleverest sheepdog in the world," agreed Fetch. They all watched as Mitch rounded up the sheep.

"Well, I must be off," said Fetch. "Are you coming to the pet show?"

"We'll see you there later," said George.

Fetch hurried back to his clinic to get ready for the pet show.

"Hello, Tom," said Kara
when Fetch arrived back
at the clinic. Kara was very
busy. She was getting her little
dog, Puddles, ready for the
pet show.

But Kara and Puddles
weren't the only ones waiting
for Fetch . . .

. . . Violet Blush and her three cats were also in the waiting room!

"Hello, Mr Fetch!" said Violet, sweetly. "Now, I'm sure one of my cats will win the pet show today, but that will upset the other two. So I think you must make all three of my cats the winner!"

"But Violet," said Fetch, "you know that when I judge the pet show, I can't have favourites. I know you'd want me to be completely fair."

Fetch knew that Violet was going to be very disappointed if her cats didn't win first prize. He was beginning to wonder if being the judge would be so much fun after all!

The pet show was held on the village green. People were already preparing their pets for the competition.

Lionel Froggatt had brought his pet iguana.

"Now, Iggy," he told him proudly, "I want you to give Fetch a nice big smile when he comes to look at you!"

"Hello, Lionel!" said Violet as she came up to his table. But when Violet saw Iggy, she screamed loudly. Violet didn't like iguanas.

Violet's cats didn't like iguanas either. They tried to scratch Iggy, but he was far too quick for them and jumped out of the way.

Violet took her cats back to their table.

"Don't forget," she said to Fetch. "You must make all three of my cats the winner so the others don't get upset."

Poor Fetch! He didn't think that any of Violet's cats deserved to win because they were always so naughty.

Just then Fetch's mobile phone started to ring. It was George Moffatt. He sounded worried. He asked Fetch to come back to the farm as quickly as he could.

Fetch rushed back to Whitecliff Farm. When he arrived, he saw that everyone had gathered around Mitch the sheepdog. They looked very worried.

"Mitch went into those bushes after a stray sheep," Pippa told Fetch. "When he came out, his face started to go very red and puffy!"

Fetch scratched his head, wondering what could have happened to Mitch.

Then he noticed some bees buzzing near the bushes.

"I think Mitch might have been stung," he said.

Fetch examined Mitch's puffy face. "Ah yes, here's the sting!" he declared.

Fetch took a pair of tweezers out of his bag and carefully removed the sting.

"I'm going to give Mitch an injection to help the swelling go down," he said, "or it could be quite dangerous."

Lucy and Trevor were too scared to look when Fetch gave Mitch the injection. But it was all over very quickly and Mitch didn't seem to mind a bit.

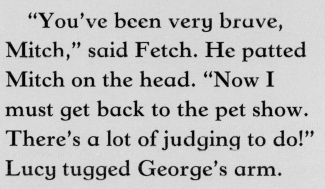

"You've been very bruve, Mitch," said Fetch. He patted Mitch on the head. "Now I must get back to the pet show. There's a lot of judging to do!" Lucy tugged George's arm.

"Can we take Trevor to the pet show now?" she asked.

"Oh, all right!" George chuckled. "We'll all go!"

Mitch jumped into George's car. He felt a lot better already.

When they reached the pet show, they could not believe what they saw. There was complete chaos!

Violet's cats were leaping everywhere, knocking over the food tables and chasing the other pets!

"My sandwiches will be ruined . . ." wailed Kara.

The only one who knew what to do was Mitch. He leapt out of George's car and started to round up the mischievous cats as if they were sheep.

Mitch chased the cats away from the tables with the sandwiches . . . and he chased them right away from all the food.

The three cats knocked over tables and chairs – there were cakes everywhere!

"Look what a mess those naughty cats have made!" said Lucy.

Mitch guided the three cats away from the tables.

He finally steered the cats back towards Violet. At last the three naughty cats were under control.

"Come to me, my little darlings," said Violet. "Is that noisy sheepdog being horrible to you?"

"Thank you, Mitch," said Kara, "you've saved my sandwiches."

"Well done, Mitch!" Pippa said as she gave him a big hug. "He really is a clever sheepdog isn't he, Mr Fetch?"

"I think Mitch saved the day," agreed Fetch. And although he examined all the pets at the show, he knew that there was only one animal that really deserved the winner's trophy.

"This year's trophy goes to a very brave and clever pet," said Fetch. "Mitch the sheepdog!"

"Well done, Mitch," said George. Everyone cheered.

"Woof, woof," barked Mitch happily.